# the little

## pictures *by esphyr slobodkina*

Copyright 1938 by William R. Scott, Inc. Copyright renewed 1966 by Roberta Brown Rauch  First published by William R. Scott, Inc.  Printed in Mexico  All rights reserved. New Edition, 1993 ISBN 0-06-021476-7.—ISBN 0-06-021477-5 (lib. bdg.)—ISBN 0-06-443389-7 (pbk.)  Library of Congress Catalog Card Number 92-17571

# fireman

## words by margaret wise brown

HarperCollins*Publishers*

once upon a time there was a

great big tall fireman

and once upon a

time there was a

little fireman

they lived in two fire houses
right next door to each other

and one fireman had a big
black and white dalmatian
puppy dog who ran behind
his fire engine to the fires

and the other fireman had a very little black
and white dalmatian puppy dog who ran to
all the fires right behind his little fire engine

one night the two firemen were

sleeping in their fire houses and

the dalmatian puppy dogs were

sleeping under their fire engines

when clang
went the loud
ringing noise
of the fire
gong in the
big fire house

and *cling!* went the

little ringing noise of

the fire gong in the

little fireman's house

bow-wow-wow

barked the big

dalmatian dog!

yip! yip! yip!

barked the little dalmatian dog!

"fire! fire! fire!"

called the people in the streets

then out from the big fire house came

the big fireman in his big fire engine

with his big dalmatian puppy

dog running behind

him

and
out from the
little fire house came
the little fireman with his little
puppy dog running along behind him

clang! clang! clang!

cling! cling! cling!

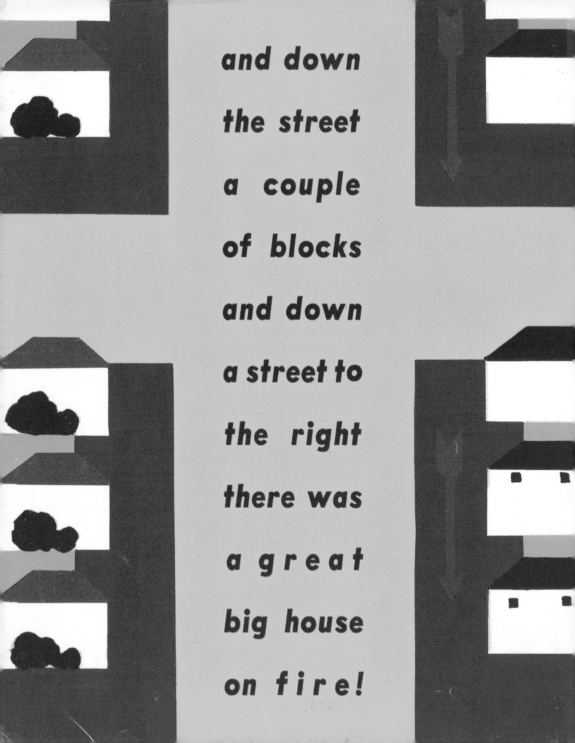

and down
the street
a couple
of blocks
and down
a street to
the right
there was
a great
big house
on fire!

when the big fireman got there, he said:

" ho! ho! what a fine big roaring fire! "

but when the little fireman got to the fire, he said:

" oh dear! oh dear! that fire is too big for me! "

and then down

the street two

blocks and on

a block to the

left he saw a

very little

house on fire!

so cling! cling! cling! off he went
down the street to the little fire

and they all
jumped out of
the windows
to the little
fireman who
caught them
in a little net

and there in
the windows of
the little house
were fifteen
little fat
ladies calling
help! help!

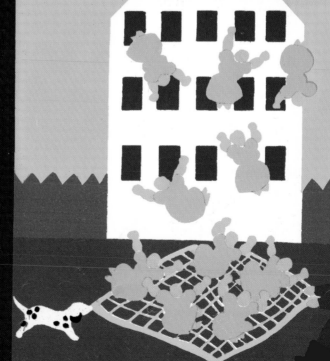

at the big fire there were fifteen
big fat ladies in the windows

and they all jumped out and the big
fireman caught them in his big net

when the big

fire was all

splashed out

with water

and when the little fire was

all splashed out with water

the two firemen jumped in their fire engines

and went home with their black and white

dalmatian

puppy dogs

running along

behind them

the big fireman ate
a great big mutton
chop and a great
big dish of pink
ice cream; then
he jumped into
bed and went
right to sleep

and the little fireman ate a
very little mutton chop and
a very little dish of pink ice
cream; then he jumped into
bed and went right to sleep

**and the great big fireman**

**dreamed** a very little dream

and

the little

fireman dreamed

a great big dream.